NOW YOU SEE ME

SUPER HUMAN

NOW YOU SEE ME

VANESSA ACTON

darbycreek

Copyright © 2018 by Lerner Publishing Group, Inc.

Darby Creek
A division of Lerner Publishing Group, Inc.
241 First Avenue North
Minneapolis, MN 55401 USA

For reading levels and more information, look up this title at
www.lernerbooks.com.

The images in this book are used with the permission of: iStock.com/Vladimirovic; iStock.com/edge6; iStock.com/nyxmedia; iStock.com/aetb; iStock.com/malija; iStock.com/sinemaslow.

Main body text set in Janson Text LT Std 12/17.5.
Typeface provided by Adobe Systems.

Library of Congress Cataloging-in-Publication Data

Names: Acton, Vanessa, author.
Title: Now you see me / Vanessa Acton.
Description: Minneapolis : Darby Creek, [2018] | Series: Superhuman | Summary: High school sophomore Tony would prefer to remain ordinary and overlooked at his school, but one day he wakes up to discover that he can literally become invisible, attracting the interest of a bully but also new friends Tony is willing to step into the spotlight to defend.
Identifiers: LCCN 2017011290 (print) | LCCN 2017035377 (ebook) | ISBN 9781512498349 (eb pdf) | ISBN 9781512498295 (lb : alk. paper)
Subjects: | CYAC: Invisibility—Fiction. | Friendship—Fiction. | High schools—Fiction. | Schools—Fiction.
Classification: LCC PZ7.1.A228 (ebook) | LCC PZ7.1.A228 No 2018 (print) | DDC [Fic]—dc23

LC record available at https://lccn.loc.gov/2017011290

Manufactured in the United States of America
1-43580-33361-6/30/2017

For MJ, the invisible genius
behind so many books!

SIXTEEN YEARS AGO, ON APRIL 12, SIX PEOPLE FROM AROUND THE COUNTRY WERE BORN WITH A HIDDEN SPECIAL ABILITY.

On their sixteenth birthday, they each develop their special ability for the first time. Whether they can soar through the clouds, run faster than the speed of light, or tear through a brick wall, all the teenagers must choose how to use their powers. Will they keep their abilities secret? Will they use them only to benefit themselves? Or will they attempt to help others—even if the risks are greater than they could imagine? One way or another, each teen will have to learn what it means to be . . . superhuman.

1

Tony didn't realize anything was different until he got to school. He'd overslept that morning and had still been half asleep when he dressed and biked over to Sasaki High. He'd been so tired that he'd left his backpack at home and had almost forgotten his phone too. Now he shuffled through the halls on autopilot, heading to his locker. At least four people had bumped into him before he started to wonder why.

He was used to being bumped into. Used to people not noticing him. It was fine, mostly. Better than being singled out as a punch line—or a punching bag. He'd had enough of that at his old school. Since transferring to Sasaki last year, he'd managed to get through all of freshman year and now most of sophomore year without attracting any attention, and it was a relief.

But seriously. How could all these people slam right into him and then look so confused, as if they hadn't seen him there?

An underclassman rushed by, his backpack clipping Tony's shoulder and knocking Tony off balance. Stumbling a little, he bumped into someone else—Shae.

Tony silently cursed himself. *Smooth, really smooth.* Shae Richards: student council president, homecoming queen, captain of the varsity volleyball team, and the nicest popular person Tony had ever met. She was friendly to everybody—*genuinely* friendly. Tony had history class with her, and she always smiled and said hi when they crossed paths.

Except today. Today she was too busy bending down to scoop up the papers she'd dropped when he'd knocked into her. Tony caught a glimpse of the multicolored, swirly type on one of the scattered pages: *SPRING FORMAL IS COMING! Dance Like No One Is Watching. Friday, April 22, 6 p.m. Buy tickets from your student council reps.*

By the time Tony knelt down to help, Shae had grabbed all the flyers. "Sorry about that," Tony said as they both stood up.

She jumped a little, then stared at him with a blank, puzzled expression. It was as if she were looking straight *through* him . . .

Was there a stain on his shirt? He hadn't looked at his clothes that closely when he got dressed this morning. He'd been too bleary-eyed after a late night of staring at his phone screen, watching old episodes of his favorite TV shows, and waiting to see if anyone else would post a "Happy birthday!" message on his wall. Well, full disclosure: waiting to see if Shae would post. Technically she followed him on social media because Shae followed *everyone* on social media, and she was the sort of person who'd wish anyone a happy birthday if she happened to see the notification. But that hadn't happened, and now they were standing face to face and . . .

Tony looked down. And saw nothing.

Correction: He saw the floor of the hallway. But not his own feet. Not any part of himself. He moved his arm toward his face—could feel it moving—but couldn't see it.

The five-minute warning bell rang, but Tony barely heard it.

Stunned, he looked back up at Shae, but she had already moved on. As he turned to see which way she'd gone, someone slammed into him from behind.

"What—" spluttered a familiar rumbling voice. Before Tony even turned around, he knew it was Erik Branson, star catcher of the varsity baseball team. His locker was down the hall from Tony's this year, and he always seemed to be having loud, intense conversations with people between classes. By now, halfway through the second semester, Tony had overheard Erik break up with two girls, bribe about eight people to do his homework for him, and threaten to get three guys kicked off the baseball team. Tony felt as if he knew the guy, even though Erik had never said a word to him—until now.

Frowning, Erik plowed straight into Tony for the second time. Tony staggered backward and grabbed Erik's arm to keep himself from falling. Then both of them stared at the same spot on Erik's arm, the spot where Tony's hand should be. It was *there*—Tony could feel his fingers clutching at Erik's sleeve—but it wasn't visible.

"Whoa," Tony blurted out.

Erik, eyes wide, flailed his arm until it came free of Tony's grip. He looked around, but by now the hallway had emptied out. Everyone else had headed to class.

"Who said that?"

"I—uh—"

"GAH!" Erik jumped back as if he'd been electrocuted. "Who's doing this? Kyle? This is not funny, man. How are you doing this?"

"I—uh—it's Tony Castellan?"

"How are you doing that? Where are you?"

"I'm right here . . ."

Without warning, Erik lunged forward and pawed at him until he got a grip on Tony's T-shirt. "What. Is. This," he said in the *don't-mess-with-me* voice that Tony overheard from a distance every day.

"I—I don't know—"

Two seconds later Erik was dragging him down the hall toward the nearest restroom. Erik shoved the door open and pulled Tony inside.

They stopped in front of the row of sinks and mirrors. Letting go of Tony, Erik said, "What do you mean you *don't know*?"

Tony gazed at the mirror in front of him, speechless. Erik's reflection glared back at him, but that was it.

Erik's voice seemed to be coming from very far away. "You're telling me you don't know how you became *invisible*?"

2

Tony could feel his chest heaving, could hear himself raggedly breathing in and out, but somehow none of it seemed real. Was *he* real? Was he alive? What had happened to him?

Erik smacked Tony.

Tony recoiled. "Hey!" The smack didn't just hurt—it seemed to send a shock wave through every cell in his body. A deep shudder ran through him, and out of the corner of his eye he saw it happen: his reflection was suddenly visible in the mirror again. When he lifted his hand to his stinging cheek, he saw his fingers, right where they were supposed to be.

His first feeling was intense relief. But almost immediately, confusion and fear crowded back into his brain. *How is this possible? What's wrong with me?*

"Ha," said Erik smugly. "Thought that might work. Just like with hiccups—the shock snaps you out of it." Then the satisfaction faded from Erik's face, and he shook his head in a mixture of disbelief and disgust. "For real, though, man. How did you do that?"

"How many times do I have to say I don't know?" Tony shouted. He realized he was shaking. Maybe from the physical jolt of whatever transformation had just happened. Or maybe just because he was freaking out. He gripped the sides of the sink to steady himself.

"Okay, okay, chill."

"Easy for you to say! You're not the one who was invisible just now!"

"Fair enough," said Erik. "Man, I wish I'd gotten video of that. One minute you weren't there and the next minute—poof! Came out of nowhere!"

"Well, I was here the whole time," Tony pointed out. "You just couldn't see me." He was still staring at his reflection in the mirror, as if *I can turn invisible!* might be stamped on his skin somewhere.

"Can you do it again?"

Tony turned away from the mirror to look at Erik. "*What?*"

"Like, can you turn invisible again?"

"I have no idea! And why would I want to? It was terrifying."

Erik shrugged. "It would be a lot less terrifying if you could control it."

"You know what would be least terrifying of all? If it never happened again, and we both forgot about it."

"Oh, right. Like I can forget there's a dude walking around my school with a superpower."

Tony had thought his stomach was already knotted to the max, but clearly he'd been wrong. Superpower? "It's—it's not a . . ." Before he could finish, the final bell rang. Tony groaned. "We're late for class. I have to go. Just—just please don't say anything about this to anyone, okay?"

Erik shrugged his broad shoulders again. "Whatever you say, Toby."

"Tony."

"Tony. Right. But hey, first, give me your phone."

Caught off guard yet again, Tony just stared blankly at Erik's outstretched hand.

Impatiently, Erik said, "So I can put my number in it. You *have* to text me if this happens again."

***

Tony watched his feet the whole time he walked to homeroom. He was about ten feet from the classroom door when he noticed his sneakers start to fade from view. At the same time, he felt some sort of ripple effect inside his body—like a shiver but somehow different, deeper. *No, no, please . . .*

Three steps later, he was fully invisible again. *Now what?* He tried slapping himself— no luck. Tony took a deep breath and considered his options.

Option one: he could text Erik. Tony fumbled for his jeans pocket and pulled out his phone. He could feel it in his hand, but he couldn't see it. Just like his clothes, it seemed to turn invisible along with his body. A fresh jolt of panic sliced through him at the thought of not being able to use his phone. But he pushed that aside, trying to focus.

Option two: he could go home. But his mom would be done with her night shift at the hospital by now, making herself a quick meal before going to sleep, and Tony couldn't imagine how she'd react to this—a son who was sometimes visible and sometimes not. She had enough to worry about.

Option three: he could . . . go to class? It seemed ridiculous, but at least it was part of a familiar routine—a little sliver of normal. He could wait in the classroom until first period was over and then find Erik again.

The door to his classroom was open, and a substitute teacher was busy writing her name on the whiteboard. Tony walked in and headed to his desk at the back of the room.

Through the chatter of the other students, he heard someone say, "She *swears* she saw a bike without a rider this morning. Just cruising right up to the bike racks by the main entrance, locking itself, and then chilling there . . ."

Great—he'd already been spotted. Sort of. *Was I invisible when I woke up this morning? I didn't really bother to look in a mirror before I left home . . . Did it happen at some point during the night?*

Once he'd sat down, he didn't know what to do with himself. He swallowed and glanced around nervously. To his left, Ryan Lockwood was texting with his phone semi-hidden under his desk. Tony envied him for being able to actually see his phone. On his right side, Janelle Moseley was writing in her notebook, as usual. He'd been wondering about that all year—who took notes in *homeroom*? What could she possibly have to write about?

More pressing question: Why had she just stopped writing and raised her head to look directly at him—or at least, at the seemingly empty space right above his chair?

All of a sudden Janelle's hand darted out, and the blunt end of her pen jabbed him in the arm.

Tony jumped, more in surprise than in pain, but then he sensed it—the shift inside him, the shivery feeling that signaled his change from invisible to visible.

Janelle blinked but didn't flinch or scream or even look all that surprised.

Tony glanced around. As far as he could tell, nobody else had been paying attention. The substitute teacher was still writing on the whiteboard, and Ryan was absorbed in texting.

"Well, that's interesting," Janelle said quietly.

Tony looked back at her. "How—how'd you know I was here?"

Janelle raised her thick, dark eyebrows at him. Those eyebrows were not playing around. "I heard footsteps coming up to the desk, and then I heard you breathing. I wasn't sure if I was dealing with a ghost or what."

Just when he'd thought he couldn't be thrown any more off balance . . . "A ghost? Do you . . . believe in ghosts?"

Janelle shrugged. "About as much as I believe in invisible people."

"*Shh!*" Tony raised a hand toward her to quiet her as he quickly glanced around the room again. "Can you keep your voice down?" he whispered.

"Literally no one is listening to us," Janelle said, not really lowering the volume of her voice. How could she be so calm, act so normal? Had she seen this kind of thing happen before?

He didn't have time to ask. "All right, people!" said the substitute briskly. "Attendance time! There should be twenty-three of you . . ." She did a quick head count. "And there are. I didn't see anyone walk in late, so I'll just count everyone as present and on time."

Well, that's one positive outcome at least, thought Tony. *Now I just have to hope I don't turn invisible again in the middle of class . . .*

Janelle had gone back to writing in her notebook. Tony couldn't help staring at her, amazed that she'd taken this in stride. He ran through a mental list of everything he knew about her: She was on student council with Shae. According to Shae's social media posts, Janelle had been a big help with planning the spring formal. But he was fairly sure Shae and Janelle weren't close friends. He only remembered seeing one picture of them together, and it was a giant group photo from last year's dance. Tony had seen Janelle sitting with her boyfriend and some other people at lunchtime, and he'd noticed her driving an ancient silver-blue car out of the school parking lot. And he'd learned a few things about her in the last minute or so: that she was quick on the uptake, that she was the opposite of melodramatic, and that she didn't get rattled easily.

A new thought wormed its way into his aching head.

Maybe she can help me.

He cleared his throat. "Um—Janelle . . .?"

She glanced over at him again, with an expression that clearly said, *Why are you wasting my valuable time?*

"Can I borrow a piece of paper? I don't have my notebook with me."

Janelle rolled her eyes but tore out a clean page from her notebook and set it on his desk.

"Thanks. Oh, uh, and something to write with?"

She sighed, fished another pen out of her bag, and leaned over to write on the page she'd just given him. *Turning invisible sure does throw you off your usual routine, huh?*

He grinned nervously. "Yeah, just a little."

Janelle pointedly held up her spare pen, then set it down so that he could write with it. For a few seconds he just held it, savoring the simple sight of his fingers. Then he wrote, *I don't know why or how this is happening. Can you help me figure it out?*

Janelle looked at the message he'd written for a long moment. Her expression was impossible to read. It occurred to Tony that she had no reason to care about what happened to him. He would just have to hope that she was curious enough about this weirdness—this *superpower?*—to look for some answers.

I can try, she wrote. *Meet me in Ms. Roman's classroom at lunch.*

Then she went back to writing in her own notebook as if this were just another ordinary day.

3

"So here's what we know." Janelle was pacing back and forth in Ms. Roman's empty classroom later that afternoon. Apparently she came here a few days a week during lunchtime to work on student council stuff. She had Ms. Roman's permission, since Ms. Roman was the student council's faculty adviser and loved overachievers. And nobody else was around—which was why she, Tony, and Erik had met up here.

Tony had made it through most of the morning without turning invisible again. But on his way to fourth period, he'd felt the flickering start up. He'd dashed to the bathroom and locked himself in a stall just in time. Then he'd stayed there for what felt like ten years, willing himself to turn back. The warning bell had given him the mental jolt he needed to rematerialize.

Now, he was visible—for the moment. He and Erik stood uncomfortably by Ms. Roman's desk while Janelle talked.

"You turn invisible sometimes. It's temporary but seems to last for varying amounts of time. When you turn invisible, so do your clothes and other things that you're carrying on you. Your phone, for instance, or a pen. But you can't turn this chair invisible by sitting in it. You can't turn the floor invisible by standing on it. It sounds like you didn't turn your bike invisible by riding it, either. I'm guessing your power is only transferable to objects that are relatively small and lightweight. And only when you're actually holding them, not just when you're touching them."

She was right about that. During his last invisibility incident, Tony had set his phone down on the restroom sink. It had immediately rematerialized, so he'd been able to text Erik to meet him and Janelle in Ms. Roman's room. As long as he didn't hold the phone in his hand, it didn't seem to be affected by just the touch of his invisible fingers. Watching the letters appear on the screen as his invisible hand tapped the touchpad had been both creepy and kind of cool—like those pianos that play on their own. When he'd finished texting and picked up the phone off the sink, it vanished.

"Okay," said Tony. "But I'm not really that interested in how it works. I just want to figure out how to undo it."

"Undo it?" yelped Erik. "You've got a *superpower* and you want to go back to being ordinary?"

"Um . . . yes?" Being ordinary was the best thing that had ever happened to him. After all those years at his old school, when he'd been called a freak for all kinds of random, stupid reasons, being ordinary was amazing.

"Well," Janelle pointed out, taking a pause in her pacing, "since we don't know what caused this to happen, we also have no way of knowing if it'll ever go away. I'm guessing you weren't hanging around any nuclear reactors or top-secret chemicals recently?"

"What? No."

She continued her pacing, ticking questions off her fingers like she was running through an ordinary checklist. "And this kind of thing doesn't run in your family?"

"Absolutely not."

"But you did just turn sixteen yesterday."

"Uh—are you stalking me?"

Janelle paused again, turning toward him. "If by 'stalking,' you mean I checked you out on social media between classes, then yes. Just trying to gather relevant information."

"And it's relevant that yesterday was my birthday?" Tony questioned as he scratched the back of his head.

"Well, this ability might be kind of like a second puberty—"

"Or a *first* puberty, judging by our hero's baby face," snorted Erik as he plopped himself into a desk chair and leaned back. It wasn't even a very good joke, but Tony recognized all the old taunts wrapped up in it. Certain guys at his old school had spent years hurling that type of joke at him.

Janelle ignored Erik's comment. "Turning invisible might just be a natural ability that you've developed at this specific point in your life. Not that much different from a growth spurt."

A new fear started to creep through Tony's veins. "Wait, so you're saying I could be this way forever?"

Janelle shrugged. "It's certainly possible. But if you learn how to control it, switch it on—and *off*—then it wouldn't have to change your life that much."

"That would be like having a killer swing and never playing baseball," Erik protested.

"Yes," said Janelle steadily. "And for someone who doesn't like baseball, that might be fine."

By now the fear was vibrating through Tony's entire body. No, wait, that wasn't fear, it was—

"And he's gone again," said Erik.

"I'm not *gone*," Tony insisted, his voice a little less steady than he would've liked. "I'm still right here."

"Well, this is a good chance for you to practice controlling the power," said Janelle. "You can figure out how to make yourself visible again—"

"But I can't do it on my own! I need someone to startle me. Someone or some*thing*."

Janelle shook her head. "If you don't want anyone else to find out about this power, you'll have to find a way to turn it off without help."

She's right, Tony thought. *And I'm used to fending for myself. I can do this. I've got to do this.* "Okay . . . give me a minute here . . ."

He tried to focus on how he felt right before the change happened—the feeling that rippled through his body, as if every particle was a wind chime being brushed by a breeze. So far, he'd snapped back into visible mode when something caught him off guard. The hiccup method, like Erik had said. But there were other ways to cure hiccups besides scaring yourself. You could hold your breath for a long time and let it out really slowly . . .

Trying not to feel like a total idiot, Tony breathed in deeply. He let the air sit in his lungs, let the pressure build until he felt like he might burst, and then—

"Whoa, nice," said Erik. "I thought it'd take you a lot longer. I was about to go grab some food from the cafeteria."

"How'd you do it?" asked Janelle.

"I, uh . . ." Tony shrugged, too embarrassed to confess how basic his method had been. "Just concentrating, you know? Like, getting in touch with my instincts."

She nodded in approval. "Well, I'm glad it worked so well. Let's see if you can use those instincts again. Try turning invisible."

"I—what? No. I don't want to turn invisible. As long as I know how to *un*-invisible myself when it happens on its own, I'm good."

"That's pretty shortsighted," said Janelle. "I think the more you practice controlling this ability, the easier it'll be for you to keep it from getting triggered at all. If that's what you want."

"Oh . . . you mean, I might learn to sense that it's about to happen and be able to stop it?"

"Yessss, that's what she meant, genius," groaned Erik. "Is this gonna take the full lunch hour? Because I am *starving.*"

"Nobody's forcing you to stay," said Janelle—and even though her usual tone wasn't exactly warm and fuzzy, Tony caught some real ice in her voice this time.

"Well, I don't want to miss anything exciting." Erik pulled out his phone. "Give it a shot, man. I bet it's not as hard as you think it is."

Yeah, and you're such an expert, Tony thought, but he kept quiet. The sooner he figured out how to shut down his ability completely, the sooner they could all forget that this whole thing had ever happened.

Except, looking at Erik, Tony had a feeling it wouldn't be that simple.

4

It turned out that Erik was right. Triggering the shift to invisibility wasn't difficult. Tony could use the deep-breathing method to make himself disappear, and then use the same method to reappear. As the end of lunch hour crept closer, Tony still wasn't sure how to prevent a shift from happening once his body decided to make the jump. But he'd made progress. At least now he wouldn't have to wait for someone or something else to jolt him out of his invisible state. He could do it himself in less than thirty seconds.

Erik was so impressed that he filmed the whole process—visible to invisible and back—on his phone. Then he grinned at Tony. "Looks like you're ready to conquer the world, my friend."

Since when are we friends? thought Tony uneasily. He still wasn't sure how he felt about having Erik film him as he went invisible, but at least it kept Erik distracted during the practice. "Um, I'll settle for not freaking anyone out in the hallways," he said. "Thanks for your help." But he was looking at Janelle when he said that.

"I mean, you have to admit," Erik went on, "this opens up all kinds of possibilities. Now that you can control how long you're invisible, you can do all kinds of things. You thinking what I'm thinking?"

"Almost certainly not," said Janelle dryly.

Erik clapped Tony on the back and grinned at him. "Girls' locker room, man."

Tony glanced from Erik to Janelle and back. "I . . . I'm not sure that would be a good idea. I don't want to—you know—violate people's privacy . . ."

"But it's *girls*!" said Erik as if Tony had somehow missed the point.

Janelle fixed him with her deadpan stare. "Girls are people too, Erik. If you'd be comfortable with an invisible lady watching the baseball team shower, good for you, but I'm sure some of your teammates wouldn't be on board with that."

Erik grimaced at her. "Don't you have student council stuff to do? Making a playlist for the spring formal or designing decorations or something?"

"Actually, there's not much left to do for the dance," Janelle said evenly. "Aside from selling the tickets, all the prep was done weeks ago. So if Tony doesn't need more input from me, I'll go eat lunch with my boyfriend." She gestured at the door with a flourish. "After you, gentlemen."

"Let's go," Erik said to Tony, practically dragging him toward the door. Tony wondered if this was how celebrities felt when their handlers were trying to keep them away from the paparazzi. He wasn't sure he liked being handled by someone he barely knew—someone like this guy.

Janelle followed them out into the empty hallway and then breezed past them, heading to the cafeteria. "Um, I guess I'll head to lunch too," Tony said, putting a little distance between himself and Erik. "Thanks for your help earlier, with the slap and everything . . ."

"Hold on, we're not done here."

Tony paused. "Uh . . . aren't we?"

"Well, like you said, I did help you out earlier. I'd say you owe me. How about a little favor? It won't be hard for you, now that you know how to control your superpower."

Right on cue, the flickering feeling started up again. But it would just be flat-out embarrassing to dematerialize in front of Erik now. Tony breathed deeply and concentrated on keeping that wavering feeling in check.

"Here's the deal," Erik went on. "My English teacher, Mrs. Morales, is giving this big test on Friday, and I'm right on the edge of failing her class. If I don't pass, I can't stay on the baseball team. So I need to nail this test."

Am I supposed to be invested in this guy's baseball career? Tony wondered, but he kept quiet.

"Here's the plan," Erik went on. "Right after school's over today, I'll get Mrs. Morales out of her classroom. While she's out of the way, all you need to do is stroll into her room, invisible, and find the answer key. Text me a picture of it, and we're all good. You won't get caught, thanks to being invisible."

"So you're asking me to help you cheat."

"Come on, don't put it like that. I'm asking you to help out a friend in need."

We're not friends though, Tony thought with a frown. *I barely even know you. And all you've really done for me is slap me in the face.* "I'm not sure I'm really . . . comfortable doing that."

Erik smirked. "Yeah, I can tell there's a lot you're not comfortable with. For example, I bet you wouldn't be comfortable with the whole world knowing about your superpower. Like, if a video of you disappearing and reappearing showed up online, and everyone at school— everyone you know, period—saw it . . . That might make you uncomfortable, am I right? All those people trying to figure out why you're different, wondering what's wrong with you.

Wondering if maybe you're dangerous."

He held up his phone. "I'm just saying, I've got a video on my phone, and I could upload it to ten different places on the Internet in two seconds if I feel like it. I wouldn't do that to a friend, of course. Not if he'd gone out on a limb for me. So what do you say, *friend*?"

I knew it was a bad idea to let him take his phone out. Tony imagined the people from his old school seeing that video. Imagined his mom seeing it. Imagined Shae seeing it . . .

"Fine," he said grimly. "You've got yourself a deal."

5

Two minutes after the bell rang at the end of the day, Tony was standing outside Mrs. Morales's classroom. He'd ducked into the restroom a few moments ago and turned invisible. Now he was waiting for Erik to show up. He pressed himself against the wall to avoid getting trampled by passing students.

Erik sauntered up to the classroom door and waited. Tony gritted his teeth and placed his hand on Erik's shoulder—maybe a little more firmly than necessary. But Erik didn't even flinch. He just smirked and gave a little nod. Then he stepped into the classroom. "Mrs. Morales? A couple of freshmen girls are giving each other black eyes at the end of the hall . . ."

"Not again," came Mrs. Morales voice from inside the room. "I'm coming. Show me where they're at . . ."

As soon as Mrs. Morales had followed Erik down the hallway, Tony made his move. He slipped through the half-open door, pushed it mostly closed behind him, and rushed over to Mrs. Morales's desk. Erik said Mrs. Morales always printed out her answer keys—he'd seen her grading tests before. So that meant she must have a hard copy of the upcoming test's key somewhere around here. Tony knew he had to work fast. Mrs. Morales would be back as soon as she found out that there wasn't actually a fight that needed to be broken up.

Six desk drawers, three binders, and nine file folders later, Tony found it: *English 10 Unit Test for April 15*. Tony slid the paper out of its folder—watching it flicker into invisibility—and set it on the desk, where it reappeared.

Next Tony took out his phone, laid it on the desk so it would turn visible, and opened up the camera app. He hovered his thumb over the camera button so that he would have a general idea of where the button was on his phone after it went invisible again. Then he picked up the phone, and it disappeared from view. His hand shook as he tried to hold the phone over the paper. *This is so wrong. It's so messed up that I'm doing this.*

He had to snap about a dozen pictures because they kept coming out blurry. The process felt as if it took ages, because each time he wanted to check an image he had to set his phone on the desk to make it reappear.

Finally he got a decent photo. After scrambling to put everything back the way he'd found it, he speed-walked out of the classroom and flung himself over to the opposite wall. He leaned against it, clutching his phone and panting, as if it were the safe zone in some stupid P.E. game. The crowd of students in the hallway had started to thin out, but plenty of stragglers were still making their way to their lockers. At the far end of the hall, Tony saw Erik talking to Mrs. Morales.

Just as he was about to send the photo of the answer key to Erik, he heard a voice next to him.

"I *thought* I heard your mouth-breathing over here."

"GAHHH." Tony looked up to see Janelle standing in front of him, arms crossed. At the same time, he felt the internal shudder that meant he had just rematerialized. He looked down to confirm. Yep, he was visible again, phone and all. Luckily, none of the other students in the hall seemed to have noticed. They were too focused on getting out of this building as quickly as possible.

"Did I catch you at a bad time?" Janelle asked dryly.

"I—uh . . ."

Tony glanced toward the end of the hallway, where Erik still stood with Mrs. Morales. The teacher looked annoyed, while Erik shrugged apologetically. Tony could hear him even from here: "Girls, am I right? One minute they're tearing each other's hair out, the next minute, they've disappeared! Like ninjas."

Way to insult girls AND ninjas in the same sentence, Tony thought. Just then, Erik looked over and saw him. He raised his eyebrows— which was somehow a much more threatening gesture than Janelle raising her eyebrows. Tony nodded as if to say, *Yeah, I got it.*

Erik smirked and returned the nod. At the same time, Mrs. Morales shook her head and turned back toward her classroom. Tony headed for the opposite end of the hall, brushing past Janelle and not stopping until he'd turned a corner. The last thing he needed was for Mrs. Morales to notice him hanging around her classroom.

Once he was in the clear, he paused to read the text Erik had just sent him: *Where's my photo?*

Tony sighed and pulled up the image again so he could send it to Erik's phone.

"Hey." Janelle caught up to him and poked him in the arm, even though he was already visible. "What are you and Erik up to?"

"Nothing!" Tony said with an overly dramatic shrug, causing his phone to slip out of his sweaty hand.

Janelle bent down and picked it up before he could even reach for it. "Is this a picture of—"

Tony snatched the phone away from her. "I thought you were better at minding your own business."

Janelle's jaw went rigid and her eyes got icy. "You're the one who asked for my help."

"Well, I didn't ask you to follow me around and look at photos on my phone, did I? That's not what I'd call helpful behavior. Staying out of my way at this particular moment would be helpful behavior."

"If you're stealing answers to a test, then staying out of your way would be the *least* helpful thing I could do for you."

Tony didn't have time to listen to her while she tried to talk him out of it. Erik was waiting on him, and Erik was not a patient guy. "Look, I didn't want to do this. Erik's forcing me. If I don't help him out, he'll upload the footage of me going invisible, and I'll be exposed."

"Come on, Tony. No one's going to believe Erik if he tells people you can make yourself invisible. And if anyone does believe him, they'll just think it's cool."

Tony shook his head. "I don't want to be cool. I just want people to leave me alone. I want to get through the rest of high school without being judged at all."

Janelle raised her eyebrows at him. "Too late for that." And for some reason, Tony felt a swoop of regret in his chest. He didn't really know Janelle, but with the way she'd handled everything today—well, he couldn't help but respect her. Knowing that she must have a pretty low opinion of him hurt more than he would've expected.

But I can't let people find out about this, he thought with a fresh surge of panic. *Most people won't react the way Janelle did. And even if they do think it's cool—they'd probably just try to use me, the way Erik's using me right now. I'm stuck.*

"Sorry, Janelle," he said, just before he pressed send on his phone. He expected her to say something snarky as he walked away, but she didn't say anything.

Somehow that was worse.

6

Tony spent the next two days being invisible as often as possible. It was the best way to steer clear of Erik. The last thing he wanted was for Erik to demand another "favor" from him. So he avoided his locker and turned invisible when he walked through the halls between classes. At lunch on Thursday, he wandered invisibly around the cafeteria, snatching bits of food off people's trays when they weren't looking.

Roaming the cafeteria was actually kind of fun. Usually he sat by himself at one end of a long table of misfits. Nobody bothered him, but nobody talked to him either. On Thursday he was able to hear dozens of conversations.

By the end of the lunch hour he knew who had broken up with whom, who was going to the dance with whom, who had gotten suspended recently and why . . . It was even better than social media.

Maybe he could get used to this invisibility thing after all.

On Friday he tried a refined version of this strategy. Near the cafeteria entrance, student council reps had set up a table where they were selling tickets to the spring formal. Shae and Janelle were manning the table today. Tony felt a pang of guilt when he saw Janelle, but it didn't last long because Shae immediately captured all his attention. He stood near the table watching her happily chat with the students who came over to buy tickets. She'd make small talk with each person as Janelle collected their money, made change, and placed the cash in a small cashbox. Then Shae would hand each student a ticket while Janelle put another tally mark in her notebook. Tony was astounded at how easily Shae talked to people—jock, nerd, and everyone in between.

Every student who came by the table left with a ticket and the warm glow of Shae's friendliness.

Toward the end of lunch hour, students had pretty much stopped coming over to the student council table. With business slowing down for the day, Shae nibbled at her lunch and turned her conversational charms on Janelle.

" . . . Yeah, Elissa and Julia and I are all chipping in to get a limo . . ."

"A limo?" said Janelle. "You're taking a limo to a dance that's held at the school gym?"

"Well, nobody in our group has a car!" Shae responded. "Are you and Steve going to show up in that adorable junk pile of yours?"

"It's not adorable, and it's not a junk pile, and yes, we are. Seriously, though, a whole limo for just the three of you?"

"Plus Elissa's and Julia's dates."

Tony stared at Shae, stunned. *Does that mean she doesn't have a date? How could someone as amazing as Shae not have a date?*

"I can't wait until I finally get my license, though," Shae went on. "I've been saving up for a car since I was twelve. I know exactly what kind of car I want . . ."

And now she'd lost him. Tony had never really understood the appeal of cars. Bikes were way more fun—not to mention less dangerous and better for the environment . . .

"It'll be amazing to finally have a car. Whenever I get stressed I'll just hit the highway and go for a joy ride."

"Just make sure you never get stressed during rush hour," said Janelle.

"I'm going to name my car Amelia." Seriously, she was still talking about cars? "What's your car's name, Janelle?"

"Um, Car. Hey, are you good here by yourself for the last ten minutes? I'd like to run to the bathroom and then grab some food."

"Yeah, sure, go ahead. I'll hold down the fort here."

Janelle handed her a small key. "Just lock up the cashbox when you're done and bring everything back to Ms. Roman."

"Yep, I'll guard it with my life," Shae joked.

"Great, thanks." Janelle got up from the

table and walked past the spot where Tony was standing. As she passed him, she grabbed his hand, dug her nails into the palm, and pulled.

Tony let out a small yelp of surprise but managed to hold off a switch to visibility. Janelle kept her arm firmly at her side, so that no one looking at her would guess she was dragging an invisible weight behind her. Tony let Janelle pull him out of the cafeteria.

Once they were out in the empty hallway, away from the cafeteria doors, Tony thought about rematerializing. But he decided not to. He felt a little less uncomfortable talking to Janelle while he was invisible. Less pathetic.

"What was that about?" he demanded, hoping he sounded more annoyed than nervous.

Janelle looked him directly in the eye, even though she couldn't see his eyes. "Just wanted to offer a quick word of advice, Castellan. You might want to try being less of a creep."

"I—uh—I didn't mean to be creepy . . ."

Janelle might as well have had *I don't have time for this nonsense* written across her forehead. "Pro tip, sir: Invisibly eavesdropping on the girl you like is creepy. Even when she's not in the locker room. Your breathing is louder than you think."

Tony felt the tips of his ears burning. He was glad he'd stayed invisible so that Janelle wouldn't see how mortified he was. "Yeah, I . . . guess I didn't think it through. I just—I like her, you know?"

"Then why don't you try actually talking to her? While you're visible."

He shrugged. "I'm not exactly great at conversation."

"I noticed. But a lot of things can be improved by practice. And liking someone from a distance isn't really the same as liking someone for real."

"What do you mean, *for real*?" he shot back, not sure whether to feel more offended or confused. "I do like her for real."

"You like a person for real when you actually *know* the person, Tony. So all I'm saying is, quit spying on Shae and start getting to know her."

Tony sighed. Janelle clearly had no clue how it felt to be anxious around other people. She probably hadn't been tongue-tied since the day she started talking. Changing the subject, he asked, "Okay, but seriously, how are you so good at knowing when I'm around? Do *you* have some kind of super-sense?"

Janelle rolled her eyes. "I just pay attention to things. I watch and listen and file things away in my brain for later. It's a useful life skill. And—" She paused, seeming slightly hesitant for the first time. Then she shrugged and went on, "I'd like to be a detective someday."

"Like with the police?"

"Maybe, or maybe a private investigator. Anyway, taking note of your surroundings is pretty critical for a job like that. I'm trying to train myself to be a good observer."

"Well, I'd say it's working. You're way better at observing than I am."

"That's a low bar," said Janelle dryly, but her mouth quirked up in a small smile.

Tony cleared his throat. "Hey, listen, about the other day . . ."

"I didn't get you in trouble, if that's what you're worried about."

"Oh—no, that wasn't what I—I mean, I would've known by now if I were in trouble. I just wanted to—well, I guess apologize?"

"You've got no reason to apologize to *me*," said Janelle with a shrug. "I'm not your conscience."

"Well, I do feel bad about the whole thing, but I especially wish I hadn't taken it out on you. You were really helpful, and I never even thanked you. And I shouldn't have talked to you like that when I—when you ran into me after school."

Janelle shrugged. "Look, forget it. I'm about to go back in there and eat. Where are you sitting?"

"Um . . ." Tony waved a hand awkwardly and then realized she couldn't see it. "Just wherever, I guess. I usually grab a spot at one of the corner tables."

"Might look a little conspicuous if you're planning to stay invisible all through lunch. Trays of food don't usually eat themselves."

"Oh . . . yeah . . . I was kind of thinking I'd just skip the eating part today."

"That's ridiculous. It's taco day—who passes up tacos? Come on, you can sit at my table and sneak bites from everybody's trays. I'll keep the others distracted so they don't notice."

***

For the last seven minutes of lunch, Janelle sat with her boyfriend, Steve, and about five other friends at a small round table—not a Cool People Table, but fairly respectable. Tony circled the table like an awkward invisible shark, snatching up bite-sized pieces of food whenever someone wasn't paying attention. And everyone was talking so much that hardly anyone was concentrating on eating. Which probably explained why they all still had food on their trays so close to the end of lunch hour.

"Just think about it," Steve was saying. "You can use 3D printers for anything these days. We could print enough food to feed every hungry person in the world. We could print organs—hearts, lungs, whatever—for people who need them. I'm telling you, if like a *fraction* of military spending went toward developing 3D printing . . ."

"Janelle, make him stop," said the guy next to Janelle.

"I make a point not to mess with anyone's free will, Darren," said Janelle. "Unless they're actively causing harm."

"He interrupted our spring formal post-party planning to talk about 3D printing. If that doesn't count as actively causing harm, I don't know what this world's coming to."

"We don't need a post-party, Darren. We do potentially need 3D printing. I'm with Steve on this one."

"No offense, Janelle," said one of the girls at the table, "but there's no point in going to the spring formal if we don't have a party after. It doesn't even have a decent theme this year. 'Dance like no one is watching'? Who thought of that?"

"Don't look at me. I wasn't on the theme committee."

"Wait, there were committees? Which one were you on?"

"The Giving Back committee. If we sell more than a certain number of tickets, we'll give the extra money to a local charity. I helped set our sales goal and pick the charity."

"Niiiiice," said someone else. "Let me guess which charity. Humane Society! No, the food shelf . . ."

Darren groaned and put his head on the table. "And this is how the last precious minutes of lunchtime slip away. With our party unplanned . . ."

What a weird group of people, thought Tony as he chewed on a stolen tater tot. And yet he found himself oddly curious about their plans for after the dance. And about 3D printing. A few times he got so wrapped up in the random tangents of their conversation that he almost went visible by accident. When the bell rang to signal the end of lunch hour, Tony watched the group scatter. Just for a moment, he wondered what it would be like to share their table for real.

7

Tony couldn't be invisible all the time. He couldn't just materialize in the middle of a classroom, already sitting at his desk. And he couldn't disappear as soon as he stepped out into the hallway. He had to find a group of people to blend in with—then flip his switch before any of them noticed.

He was just about to do that on Monday afternoon, on his way to lunch, when he ran into Erik. "Hey, Tony. Let's talk."

Erik grabbed him by the arm before Tony could figure out an escape route.

"You know that test you were supposed to help me out with? The answer key you gave me didn't match the questions at all. I guess Mrs. Morales decided to change everything at the last minute. Any idea why she would do that?"

Tony fought to keep his expression neutral. If only he were invisible right now. "I . . . can't imagine."

"Well, I can imagine. I can imagine that someone tipped her off that one of her students was planning to cheat."

"It wasn't me!"

"Then who else could it have been?"

Tony swallowed back an *I don't know.* Janelle—it had to be Janelle. She must've talked to Mrs. Morales. *She did what I should've done. Why didn't I think of that?*

There was no way Tony could rat her out.

Erik loosened his grip on Tony's arm and gave him a fake smile. "Look, man, don't worry about it. You can make it up to me. You know how student council's selling tickets to the dance?"

"Yeah . . ."

Erik lowered his voice. "Well, I'll feel a lot better about failing that test if you can slip some of the money out of the student council cashbox."

Great, now he wants me to steal for him. And I wouldn't just be stealing from student council—from Shae and Janelle—I'd be stealing from that charity that's supposed to get some of the money.

More than anything, Tony wished he could just turn invisible and slip out of Erik's grasp. But Erik would find him again eventually.

Besides, the next time Tony saw Janelle, he wanted to be able to look her in the eye.

"You know what? No."

Erik glowered at him. "Excuse me?"

"It's *seeing* me that gets tricky sometimes, not hearing me."

Erik's lip curled in a sneer. "Real cute." He took out his phone and brandished it in Tony's face. "In that case, say goodbye to your life as an ordinary loser. And say hello to your life as a *freak* loser."

Great comeback, Tony thought, but he couldn't bring himself to say anything. He just watched as Erik pressed a button on his phone, sharing his secret with the world.

8

Tony stayed visible as he walked into the cafeteria. By the time he'd gotten through the food line, he could tell that at least half the people in the room had seen the video.

So many faces were turned toward him, so many eyes staring. Most people were trying to be subtle and spoke in whispers or talked behind their hands. But a few were straight out pointing at him. The cafeteria was always loud, but now the noise was at a roar.

Tony clutched his tray and looked around for a safe place to sit—some corner where no one would bother him. But random people were already coming up to him.

"Hey, are you the guy in this video?"

"It's totally him! How did you do this? It's not real, is it?"

"Is it real?"

"Uh, no, no, it was all just a joke . . . special effects . . . definitely not real." Tony found himself repeating the same denial over and over again as people kept approaching him. Finally he wrapped up his burrito, stuffed it in his sweatshirt pocket, dumped the rest of his tray, and left the cafeteria.

This wasn't the first time he'd eaten lunch in a locked restroom stall. Before he'd come to Sasaki High School, he'd spent a lot of time hiding out from certain people.

The kind of attention he was getting today ought to feel different. After all, Janelle had been right—a lot of people seemed to think his invisibility was cool. Or at least amusing, since most of them probably didn't believe the video was real. Yet he still felt the urge to hide. He turned invisible inside the stall, taking bites out of the invisible burrito in his invisible hands.

It was probably pretty messed up that he wanted to be invisible even when no one was around to see him. Was he hiding from *himself*?

***

Visible again, Tony stopped at his locker before his next class. Someone tapped him on the shoulder, and when he turned to see who it was, he almost shifted into invisibility from the surprise.

It was Shae. "Hey, Tony, I just wanted to say I think what Erik Branson did to you was stupid and petty. I guess that's his idea of a high-concept joke—to make you look literally invisible. I just wanted you to know that Erik doesn't speak for all of us, and you're not invisible."

Tony's chest swelled. This might be the sweetest thing anyone had ever said to him. He opened his mouth to thank her, and what came out was, "Actually, I *can* turn invisible."

Shae stared at him. "I . . . don't think I'm following you."

Why had he said that? He should take it back, pretend she'd heard him wrong. But instead he found himself whispering, "The video is real. I really can do that. I . . . can show you if you'd like."

Three minutes later Tony and Shae were standing in a deserted corner of the school library. Tony took a deep breath. *I can't believe I'm doing this . . .* "Okay, here we go."

He turned invisible, and Shae gasped. After waiting about ten seconds, he switched back.

Shae's eyes were shining—even more than usual. "That is *amazing.*"

"Um, thanks. It's not like I can take that much credit for it. It just kind of happened to me. And I'd really feel more comfortable if people didn't know about it. So can you kind of . . . not mention that I showed you?"

"Oh, of course! If anyone asks me, I'll say I can neither confirm nor deny."

"Um, okay. Or feel free to just deny."

"Oh." She let out an embarrassed laugh. "Yeah, sure. I was just quoting *Willson & Peale.* You know, the crime show?"

"Not a big fan of crime shows, actually—sorry. I'm more into comedies. *County Records. Friendzoners* . . ."

She wrinkled her nose, just briefly, but he caught the gesture of distaste. How could anyone dislike *Friendzoners*? "Oh, no problem. Sorry my joke didn't make sense."

"Oh, it's fine. Thanks for covering for me."

"Thanks for trusting me. Guess I'd better get to class." She smiled at him again before walking off, but it didn't have the same effect it usually did. They'd just shared a moment that should've felt special, and it had just been uncomfortable.

Really, though—who didn't like *Friendzoners*?

9

After school, Tony was heading toward the bike rack in front of the main entrance when a group of guys surrounded him.

There were five of them. Tony recognized a couple guys who were on the baseball team with Erik. Not especially big guys, but they definitely had more muscle than Tony did. They formed a tight ring around him.

"So this is the dude who can turn invisible," said one snarly-voiced guy.

"Supposedly," scoffed one of the others. "Let's see you do it, man."

"Yeah," said a third guy. "Show us how it works."

Tony couldn't speak—couldn't move—couldn't do anything. Turning invisible wouldn't be much help right now. These guys had formed such a tight circle around him that they'd still know exactly where he was, and he'd never have a chance to break free.

"I bet he faked the whole thing. Just looking for attention."

"Yeah, and tricking our boy, Erik."

Tony managed to find his voice. "Erik's the one who faked it."

"You talking smack about Erik now? Want us to show you what happens to people who mess with Erik?"

This had happened so many times before he came to Sasaki High. Tony knew what would happen next. He'd never been good at fighting—had never *wanted* to be good at it. So he would grit his teeth, try to protect his most vulnerable spots, and wait it out.

The sound of screeching tires broke everyone's concentration.

Janelle Moseley's battered-up silver-blue car rattled to a stop about a hundred feet away.

Janelle leaned out of the driver's window. "Hey, Kyle, shouldn't you be at baseball practice? I thought those afternoon training sessions were supposed to fix your losing streak."

"You stay out of thi—" one guy started to say.

But by then, Tony had switched. And he was charging forward, plowing into the narrow gap between two of his attackers. Both guys were knocked aside by the force of the impact, and Tony kept running.

"Where'd he go?"

"He was right there, come on—"

Tony ran full tilt toward Janelle's car and crashed straight into the back passenger door.

"It's unlocked!" Janelle shouted at him, and sure enough, as he fumbled with the handle, the door opened. He slid in just as Janelle stepped on the gas. The car peeled away, leaving the five goons to run after it for a few feet before they gave up.

By the time Tony caught his breath, Janelle had pulled out of the parking lot. The car sailed down the street, making several noises cars weren't supposed to make. Tony's heart rate gradually slowed, and he let himself rematerialize in Janelle's backseat. That's when he realized that Janelle wasn't the only other person in the car. Steve was sitting in the front seat.

"What in the name of what-ness," said Steve, craning around to look at Tony. "I mean, what in the living *what*?"

"Steve, this is Tony Castellan, a.k.a. Mr. Invisibility," said Janelle with her eyes on the road. "Tony, this is my boyfriend, Steve Park."

"Nice to meet you," Tony gasped out. "And thanks for that."

"I can't believe this," said Steve. "He really does turn invisible. And he *still* needed us to rescue him."

"Steve," Janelle sighed, "no need to be so harsh."

"I'm just saying—the guy's got a superpower, and people are still able to gang up on him?"

"Hey, it's not my fault!" Tony blurted out. "It's not like I have super-strength or armor-skin or, I don't know, the ability to fly. Invisibility doesn't give me any advantage in a fight. It's the least cool, least useful superpower ever."

Steve and Janelle glanced at each other. Then Steve said, "Yeah, that's fair."

"You won't tell anyone else, will you?" Tony asked Steve. "I've been trying really hard to convince everyone that Erik's video of me is just a fake."

"Most people won't need much convincing of that," said Janelle. "And of course Steve won't tell anyone what he just saw. Neither will those guys back there, I'm guessing. Not unless they want to admit how easily you got away from them."

Tony leaned his head back and closed his eyes. "I never wanted this, you know. I never wanted to be some kind of freak."

"Oh, come on," said Janelle impatiently. "You're not a freak."

"But I'm not normal."

"There's no such thing as normal." She said this so offhandedly that Tony knew she wasn't just trying to make him feel better. She really believed it.

"So now what do I do?"

Janelle met his eyes in the rearview mirror. "Are you asking me?"

"Yeah. I mean, I know you don't owe me any help, especially not after everything you've already done. But I'd really like to know what you think."

Another pause. Then Janelle said, "I think you go home and have a quiet, relaxing night. And then I think you should start sitting with us at lunch. If you want to."

Tony let out a long breath. Janelle was on his side—and if she trusted Steve, Tony would trust him too. Maybe he did have the least useful superpower ever, but at least it wasn't the only thing he had going for him.

10

By Tuesday morning, everyone had pretty much forgotten about the video.

Or at least everyone was focused on more important things. Some senior girl had made an online dating profile for her dog and was live-blogging actual dates that the dog went on—with humans. And several people had gotten video footage of the geography teacher performing sad love songs at a café.

Tony stayed visible all day, but he might as well have been invisible. Most people paid no attention to him—aside from Janelle, Steve, and their friends, who welcomed Tony to their table, no questions asked. Tony didn't say much, but it felt good to be sitting with these people, hearing them talk, not feeling judged or threatened. He sat with them all week, and gradually he stopped wishing he was invisible—at least during lunchtime.

On Friday, he walked into the cafeteria and spotted Shae sitting at the student council ticket table. She gave him a little wave, and he found himself walking over to the table.

"Hey, Shae . . ."

She smiled brightly at him, as usual. "Hi, Tony! What's up?"

"Uh, how are the ticket sales going?"

"Awesome, actually! We've passed our goal, which means we'll be able to donate some of the profits to the Truth and Dare Foundation. That's a charity that helps sick kids. And there may still be some last-minute ticket purchases today."

"That's great. You, uh, looking forward to tonight?"

"Yeah, my friends and I are getting a limo and I'm *so* stoked to ride in a limo . . ."

"Right, well, uh, I was wondering . . . like, do you have a date?"

"Oh, no, I'm just going with my friends."

"Would you, uh, maybe like to go with me?"

Shae blinked, and her mouth suddenly seemed torn between her usual friendly smile and an apologetic grimace. Tony's heart instantly plummeted into his small intestine. "Oh . . . thanks, Tony, that's really flattering, but I don't think so. You're a super sweet guy, but I just don't think of you like that. I'd be happy to sell you a ticket for the dance, though!"

"Um, no thanks . . ." Now would be a great time to turn invisible, except that would make the moment even *more* embarrassing. "See ya."

He dragged himself over to Janelle's table, thinking back to what Shae had said in the library. *So much for me being amazing.*

***

"Steve," Janelle said around a bite of her sandwich, "tell him to snap out of it."

"Tony," said Steve, "snap out of it."

Tony slumped in his chair. So far it was just him, Janelle, and Steve at the table. "Clearly neither of you have ever been rejected before."

Steve snorted. "You should've been here in eighth grade. I asked Darren out—obviously this was before I was going out with Janelle, and before Darren was with Leo. He shut me down sooooo fast. It was brutal."

"Yeah, but Steve handled it with class," added Janelle. "And now we're all friends."

"Well, I'm sorry I don't have as much maturity as thirteen-year-old Steve Park," said Tony a little sullenly. "Can't I be upset that Shae turned me down? On Monday . . ." He lowered his voice even though the rest of the group hadn't arrived yet. "I showed Shae my power. She's the only person I've shared it with on purpose. And I thought . . . well, I thought she was starting to see me differently."

Janelle sighed. "Shae doesn't owe you anything just because your superhuman ability makes you more memorable than before. If she's not into you as a person, then that's the way it is. You have to respect that."

"And be grateful she's not the kind of person who would want to be with you *just* because you can bend the laws of physics,"

Steve added. "That situation would have 'toxic relationship' written all over it."

"I'm not saying I want to *marry* her," sulked Tony. "I just wanted a date for the dance!"

"Dates for dances like this are overrated," said Janelle. "No offense, Steve."

"None taken. She's right, Tony—aside from, like, two slow dances it doesn't really matter if you've got a date. You could totally come and hang out with our group."

Tony managed to smile. "I'm good, thanks. I appreciate it, though, guys—really."

"Time for you to get your mind off Shae," said Steve. "How about putting your superpowers to good use by figuring out what kind of revenge plot Erik's planning against Janelle."

Tony sat up in his chair. "Wait, what? Revenge on Janelle?"

Janelle rolled her eyes. "He's being melodramatic," she told Tony.

"Steve or Erik?" he asked.

"Both of them, probably."

Steve shook his head and pulled out his phone. "Look at this, though." He held the phone toward Tony, who leaned over to see the screen. Erik had written a post online, and even though he didn't identify the person he was talking about, it was pretty clear: *You'll be sorry you ratted me out. I have a plan. Better watch your back.*

Tony looked back at Janelle. "You think he figured out you were the one who told Mrs. Morales about his plan to cheat?"

"Seems that way," she said. "It wouldn't be hard to figure out, even for someone as dense as Erik. He did see you talking to me right after you went into Mrs. Morales's classroom that day." She didn't seem fazed, but Tony felt sick to his stomach. The idea of Erik going after Janelle because she'd done the right thing when Tony hadn't dared . . .

"It's not a big deal," Janelle insisted. "He's all talk."

"I'm not sure that's true." Tony felt himself starting to flicker inside. He mentally clamped down on the impulse to disappear. "And it wouldn't hurt to keep an eye on him, just in case."

"My thoughts exactly," said Steve. "And the best person to keep an eye on him . . ."

Tony finished the sentence: ". . . Is someone he can't see."

11

Tony stayed after school to watch the baseball team practice, not moving from his seat until they finished at five that evening. *Good thing Mom's still working the night shift and won't know I'm not home*, he thought as he watched Erik and the other guys run through their plays. *She'd never believe me if I told her I was late because I'd been invisibly stalking my worst enemy.*

Erik didn't say anything shady during practice. Tony let the baseball jargon wash over him and tried to relax. Maybe he and Steve had overreacted. Erik probably didn't have some master plan to ruin Janelle's life. He was just a jerk who didn't know how to shut up.

Still, Tony shadowed the team back to the locker room after practice. The guys' locker room wasn't exactly familiar territory for him. The first thing he noticed was how much it echoed. Every invisible step he took seemed to fill the whole space. Maybe he should've taken off his shoes . . . but it was too late for that now.

Once the guys had showered and gotten dressed, most of them headed out. But a couple of them hung around the lockers. Tony recognized them from the group that had tried to jump him after school last Friday. They waited until everyone else was gone, then huddled around Erik.

"Listen up, guys," said Erik. "I'm only going to say this once."

An idea hit Tony straight in the gut. He wasn't sure what made him think of it— probably Erik's previous stunts. Slipping to a different row of lockers, Tony quietly pulled out his phone and set it on a bench so he could see it. He found the audio recording feature and pressed Start as he tiptoed back to where Erik and his friends stood.

"So here's what's going to happen," Erik told his goons in a loud whisper. The guy really didn't know how to keep his voice down. "I'll steal the student council cashbox. It's in Ms. Roman's classroom. I've seen where she keeps it. I'll make it look like Janelle took it. You guys will back me up."

Wait, what? thought Tony. *How is he going to frame Janelle for this? Seriously, THIS is his master plan?*

Erik certainly seemed confident, though. "She'll be expelled before she knows what hit her. And nobody will be able to do anything about it, including Castellan. So much for that guy being superhuman, right?"

One of the guys—Kyle?—chuckled. The other one said, "We've got your back, Branson." Tony crept back to the other row of lockers and set his phone on the bench once more. He hit stop on the recording feature and started swiping at his phone. He sent the file with the recording to Janelle. Then he followed up with a text: *Not sure what this means but can't be good—*

"Wait a minute," said Erik suddenly. "I hear something . . ."

He peered around the corner of a locker block, looking right at the bench where Tony was crouching. And his eyes were locked on Tony's phone, which still sat on the bench in all its glorious visibility.

Before Tony could react, Erik dove toward the bench like he was sliding for home base. Erik's fingers closed over the phone, and Tony had to scrabble backward so that Erik's other outstretched hand wouldn't find him.

Tony leapt up and took off running.

"It's Castellan! He's in here!"

Not for long, thought Tony as he sprinted out of the locker room.

But what was he supposed to do now?

12

Erik's voice snaked up the staircase as Tony ran to the second floor.

"Heeeeeeere, TonyTonyTony. Come out, come out, wherever you are . . ."

It was only a matter of time before he used a line like that, Tony thought grimly.

He headed toward Ms. Roman's classroom, not sure what he was going to do. All he knew was that he couldn't let Erik get there first. Maybe Ms. Roman or some of the student council members would be in there, setting up for the dance. He might be able to warn them that Erik was planning to steal from them. *If only Erik didn't have my phone . . . I can't believe*

I let him grab it. Too bad my superpower wasn't amazing reflexes instead of invisibility . . .

The door to Ms. Roman's classroom was unlocked. Tony dashed in and found the room empty. He didn't flip on the lights, since Erik was probably right behind him.

He couldn't let Erik get to the cashbox. *If I had super-strength, I could fight him off,* Tony thought. *If I had mind-control abilities, I could convince him to ditch his whole plan. But being invisible won't stop him.*

Unless I take the cashbox myself.

He could keep the cashbox away from Erik. At least until he found someone responsible to take charge of it.

Finding the cashbox wasn't hard. It was in the top drawer of Ms. Roman's desk.

Tony carefully tucked the cashbox under his jacket, holding it tight against his chest. It disappeared, just like his phone disappeared while it was in his jeans pocket.

Ugh, Erik still has my phone.

But he had bigger problems to worry about at the moment.

Like the fact that Erik could walk into this classroom at any moment.

Like the fact that Erik and his two goons were now standing in the classroom doorway, blocking his exit.

"You in here, Castellan?" said Erik. "Come on, don't be shy."

Tony knew he was trapped. He stood as still has he could, hardly even breathing, convinced that the slightest noise would give away his location.

"Well, that's all right," Erik said, his eyes scanning the room. "My man Kyle is just going to stand here blocking the door while Wyatt and I have a look around."

Create a distraction, Tony told himself. Erik hadn't bothered to turn the lights on, so the classroom was still pretty dark. *Chances are if I pick something up, Erik won't see it disappear. And even if he does . . .*

He'd have to risk it.

Tony grabbed a pen from the jar on Ms. Roman's desk and hurled it at the far corner of the room. It hit the wall with a small but distinct clatter, and Erik's head snapped toward the noise. "Think you can hide from me, Castellan?" he shouted, lunging toward the back wall. One of the other guys followed him, leaving Kyle to guard the door.

Now or never, Tony thought. He ran for the door, hoping to squeeze past Kyle without him even noticing—

Kyle must have heard his footsteps. His arm shot out and sideswiped Tony. Tony flailed his own arms defensively, and both he and Kyle went down. Tony landed hard on his shoulder. Kyle landed on top of him, so it looked as if he was hovering a few feet off the ground.

It turned out that Tony had been wrong when he'd said invisibility gave him no advantages in a fight. When the guy wrestling with you can't see you, you definitely have an edge. Even if you've only got one free arm because your other arm is curled around a bulky stolen cashbox.

Kyle didn't see the fingers shooting up to jab at his face, or the knee coming for his groin. Kyle was fighting blind. All Tony had to do was land a few solid blows—nothing that would hurt Kyle badly, but enough to throw him off balance. Then it was easy enough for Tony to wriggle free of Kyle's grip and take off running down the hallway.

He'd made it about thirty feet before he heard Erik yelling behind him, "Get him! Come on!"

Tony was about to speed up, but then he remembered how Janelle always knew where he was because she could hear his footsteps and breathing. And with the cashbox rattling around at his side, he'd be making even more noise than usual.

If Erik and the others could hear Tony up ahead of them, they'd have a fairly easy time tracking him.

So Tony stood still.

Erik and the others blazed past him. Halfway to the end of the hall, Erik shouted, "Split up! Kyle, go back the other way! He's close!"

Kyle turned around and ran back, passing Tony again on his way to the other end of the hall. A moment later, all three of Tony's chasers were gone. The hallway was empty.

He let out a long breath and almost flickered back into visibility, but he caught himself just in time.

He glanced at a clock on the wall. It was past six. The dance must've started by now. Pretty much everyone on student council would be there, plus plenty of teacher chaperones. If he could find Janelle or Shae, he could give the box to one of them, and they could handle things from there.

Tony headed for the gym.

***

Two teachers stood in front of the gym entrance, collecting tickets from students in black suits and flashy dresses. Tony spotted Ms. Roman but didn't know how to approach her. *Here, I stole this cashbox to keep someone else from stealing it?* Better to find Janelle or Shae, since they would actually trust him.

The line of students slowly moved forward, trading their tickets for entry to the gym.

Tony automatically thought, *How will I get in? I don't have a ticket.* And then he followed that thought with, *You idiot, you don't need a ticket— you're invisible!*

Still practicing his best stealth-walk, he slipped past Ms. Roman and walked through the open double doors. He heard Ms. Roman say to Mr. Hudson, the other teacher taking tickets, "Can you cover for me for a minute? I just need to run back to my room and grab something . . ."

Better work fast, Castellan—before she realizes the cashbox is missing.

The gym looked like—well, like the gym. The student council members had done their best, but streamers and balloons can only get you so far. A sparkly banner with the words *Dance Like No One Is Watching!* hung on one wall. Off to one side, the geography teacher operated a small sound system. Apparently he was the DJ. At the other end of the room stood a refreshment table and a small, rickety-looking platform with a standing microphone on it. Round tables from the cafeteria were set up nearby. But most students were gathered in the open area, dancing in pairs and larger clumps. *At least I haven't been missing out on much*, Tony thought.

He was looking around for Shae or Janelle when he heard Erik's voice behind him. "I've got a ticket!"

"I see that, young man, but you're going to have to wait your turn in line," Mr. Hudson said.

Okay, thought Tony, *better work even faster.*

He wove through the crowd of dancers, trying not to make any noise whenever someone stepped on his invisible feet. Finally, he spotted Janelle dancing in a circle with Steve and the rest of their friends. He barely recognized her in that shimmery dress, with her hair down and makeup on.

As he moved toward Janelle, Tony noticed Shae sitting at one of the tables with her friends. There was nothing surprising about how Shae looked—she was just a slightly fancier version of her usual gorgeous self. Tony paused and forced himself to focus. Should he give the box to Shae or to Janelle? Since Shae was student council president and Janelle was just a member, maybe he should give the box to Shae. Plus, no one was trying to frame Shae for stealing the box, so it wouldn't look suspicious for her to have it . . .

Just then, Ms. Roman dashed onto the little stage and grabbed the microphone. "I need everyone's attention, please!"

The music cut off. Students reluctantly fell silent and stood still.

"I'm afraid there's been a theft," said Ms. Roman grimly. Surprised murmurs rose from the crowd of students. "The cashbox containing the money from this dance's ticket sales is missing. That's hundreds of dollars in cash. You, the student body, entrusted that money to student council members. And it seems that someone has taken advantage of your trust. No one is leaving this gym until we find that cashbox and account for all the money in it."

Now the murmuring took a more outraged turn.

Tony felt the hard lump of the cashbox under his jacket. *This could get awkward.*

And right on cue, he heard Erik's unmistakable voice. "Someone should ask Janelle Moseley about that!"

Heads turned. Hundreds of eyes darted from Janelle, who stood with her friends near the stage, to Erik, who stood with his two goons just inside the gym entrance.

"I heard her bragging that she could steal student council money without getting caught," Erik declared. His voice echoed off the gym's high ceiling.

"That's ridiculous," said Janelle flatly. Her voice carried pretty well too. She had more powerful lungs than Tony had realized.

"You had access to the cashbox, didn't you?" Erik shot back.

"Yeah, and so did every other student council member who sold dance tickets over the past month. But I didn't go near Ms. Roman's room at any point today, Erik. I wasn't on ticket sale duty at lunch. I don't have Ms. Roman for class. And I'm not on the Setup

Committee that stayed late today to get the gym ready for the dance. I went home when school let out at three, and when I came back for the dance I went straight here."

"It doesn't matter if you didn't go near the box earlier today," Erik snapped. "The box disappeared sometime in the last hour."

"How do you know that?"

Erik blinked. "Ms. Roman just said so."

Ms. Roman was looking back and forth between Janelle and Erik. "I . . . didn't say that, actually. But it's true. The cashbox was in its usual spot when I headed over to the gym around five thirty. It was gone when I went back to my classroom a few minutes ago."

"Which means," Erik said, his voice getting louder and more aggressive with each syllable, "Janelle could've—"

"I've been in the gym the whole time," said Janelle. "And a ton of people can vouch for that."

Erik wasn't finished, though. "Even if she didn't personally do it, she could've had someone else do it for her. She's been hanging around Tony Castellan a lot lately. Does anybody know where *he's* been tonight?"

Oh, thought Tony. *THIS was his master plan. Framing both of us. And I walked right into it.*

In the back of his mind, Tony knew it was still a pretty bad master plan. He knew he should just keep calm. He should stay invisible and wait it out. The teachers would probably believe Janelle over Erik anyway. Tony could find a way to return the cashbox later, and no one would have to know he'd been here at all . . .

Except he was tired of hiding.

"Hey, Erik! Over here."

People looked around in confusion, searching for the source of the new voice.

You idiot, Tony thought again. *You haven't rematerialized yet.*

He took a long, deep breath and felt himself turn visible. The people closest to him gasped, starting a ripple effect across the whole gym. But Tony focused on Erik, who glared at him from across the room.

Tony met Erik's eyes. "Have you been looking for me?"

13

"There he is!" Erik yelled. "And he's got something under his jacket!"

"Yeah," Tony shot back. "The cashbox *you* wanted to steal. I brought it here to keep it away from you."

Erik snorted. Everyone else gave Tony blank looks. *Yep, that sounded just as unconvincing as I figured it would.* But then he remembered they had proof. He called, "Janelle, check your phone!"

While Janelle was rooting around in her tiny clutch purse, Tony made his way over to the stage. He held up the cashbox for Ms. Roman to take. "Sorry about that, Ms. Roman—really."

"He's just trying to cover for himself now that he's been busted!" protested Erik.

A very confused Ms. Roman leaned over to take the cashbox. The crowd continued its agitated muttering.

"We can't trust him!" shouted Erik. "Didn't you all see what just happened? He was *invisible*! Guy's a total freak! And he admits he stole the cashbox—"

"Everybody listen up!" Janelle shouted over Erik, climbing onto the stage. She took the microphone from Ms. Roman and spoke into it. "Tony Castellan is not a thief. Erik Branson is. I have proof." In her free hand, Janelle held her phone up to the microphone. "I got this message at five forty-seven today. If I wasn't in the middle of the group photo op that Darren insisted on, I would've checked my phone earlier. But moving on . . ." She pressed a button, and Erik's voice echoed through the room.

" . . . *And nobody will be able to do anything about it, including Castellan.*"

Janelle paused the recording just before Erik's reference to Tony's superpower.

"Obviously," Janelle said to the teachers, "Erik is the culprit here. And Tony wasn't helping him. In fact, Tony overheard this conversation, recorded it, and sent it to me. If Tony hadn't acted quickly to keep the cashbox away from Erik, we might've lost the money."

Several teacher chaperones closed in on Erik. His two goons had vanished, blending into the crowd. *So much for having Erik's back*, Tony thought. "Erik, I think you'd better come with us," Mrs. Morales said sternly.

"Oh, and I'm going to need my phone back, if you don't mind," added Tony.

Mrs. Morales glowered at Erik. "Turn out your pockets."

"This is ridicu—"

"*Do it.*"

A moment later Mrs. Morales handed Tony's phone back to him. "It looks like Mr. Branson is guilty of two thefts."

"But he's the one who can turn invisible!" Erik shouted. "Doesn't anyone care about that?"

"Honestly, at the moment, not really," said Ms. Roman. She climbed down from the stage, clutching the cashbox to her chest.

Erik kept protesting as the teachers herded him out of the gym, but Tony had no trouble tuning him out.

Kids crowded around Tony, clapping him on the back and even shaking his hand.

"That was *epic*, man!"

"How long have you been able to do that?"

"Can you teach me how it works?"

Tony politely shrugged them off with variations of "Thanks, yeah, long story." Meanwhile, Janelle calmly reattached the microphone to its stand, gathered up her long skirt, and climbed off the stage. Steve started clapping for her, Tony joined in. A moment later everyone in the gym was applauding, though most of them weren't sure why.

The DJ-slash-geography-teacher cleared his throat and spoke into his own microphone. "Well, that was certainly interesting. Seems like now's a great time for some sad love songs . . ."

A roar of protest went up from the students, and the teacher reluctantly went back to the set playlist. Tony watched as kids started dancing again. Only a few people stared at him, still confused and curious about what they'd seen him do. Tony found that it didn't bother him, at least not at the moment. He felt amazingly calm.

"Tony!"

Shae was coming over to him, beaming. "Thank you so much for keeping the money safe."

"Oh, no problem. Well, I mean—it was kind of a problem, but I was glad to do it, you know?"

Shae's smile widened even more. "Yeah. You're a good guy, Tony."

"Thanks. You're pretty awesome too." This was it, he realized. This was his chance to ask her out. Or at least ask her to dance with him. At this point—now that he was a school hero— she might actually even say yes . . .

Except I'm not a different person than I was yesterday. I'm the same Tony, and she's the same

Shae. And now that he knew her a little better, Tony had trouble picturing himself with her. After all, she was a car enthusiast who didn't like *Friendzoners*. What would they even talk about on a date? Though he did still think she was beautiful, and sweet, and really cool. Maybe they would end up being friends. Tony wouldn't mind having a few more good friends.

"Enjoy the rest of the night," he said, and he saw her shoulders relax.

"You too, Tony."

As Shae headed back to her friends' table, Tony heard a familiar voice behind him.

"So I take it you're not going to try sweeping her off her feet?"

He turned and smiled at Janelle. "She's got her feet pretty firmly planted on the ground. At least, I think she does. Unless it turns out that she can fly. I might not be the only one at Sasaki with superhuman powers."

"That's the spirit. Don't get too convinced that you're special. Now are you planning to stand here all night basking in your victory, or what?"

"Well, I've decided something."

"Yeah? That's refreshing."

Tony let the dig slide. "You were right—I'm not cut out to be a superhero. But I think I make a pretty decent sidekick, don't you?"

Janelle grinned at him. "Actually, I do. Now come on. I didn't come here to make friends—I came here to dance!"

She led him over to Steve and the rest of her group. The others made room for him in their circle, and for the first time in his life, Tony danced like no one was watching.

FIFTEEN YEARS LATER

CHARITY TREASURER CAUGHT IN EMBEZZLEMENT SCHEME

Businessman Jared Cosgrove was arrested Thursday night and charged with embezzling funds from the Truth and Dare Foundation.

Police officers credited Dr. Janelle Moseley, private investigator, and her partner, A. T. Castellan, with assisting in the case. Dr. Moseley and Mr. Castellan obtained crucial evidence that led to Mr. Cosgrove's arrest, including recordings of Mr. Cosgrove privately discussing his plans with associates.

This is the fifth high-profile case Dr. Moseley has helped police solve this year, adding to her already extensive success record as a private detective. Mr. Castellan's expertise and specific role in the investigation are unknown.

G A SUPERPOWER IS NOT
HE COMIC BOOKS MAKE IT

CK OUT ALL OF THE TITLES

SUPER HUMAN

SERIES

D OVER MATTER   STRETCHED TOO
W YOU SEE ME   STRONGHOL
KING UP SPEED   TAKE TO THE S

WHAT WOULD YOU DO IF YOU WOKE UP IN A
VIDEO GAME?

CHECK OUT ALL OF THE TITLES IN THE

LEVEL UP

SERIES

ABOUT THE AUTHOR

Vanessa Acton is a writer and editor based in Minneapolis, Minnesota. She enjoys stalking dead people (also known as historical research), drinking too much tea, and taking long walks during her home state's annual three-week thaw.